Praise for Dangerous Shadows

Dangerous Shadows is an exciting, fast-paced read that fans of romantic thrillers will devour.

— Priscilla Evans, Managing Editor, Literary Titan

Literary Titan Silver Book Award Winner

This quick novella excites readers for more from Shittim as her enthralling characters and compelling plot pull us ever deeper. Giving us just a taste of what she has to offer, "Dangerous Shadows" leaves us craving a future for our unlikely pair.

— Jill Rey, For The Love Of The Page

Also by Amanda Shittim

Lethal Obsession

Lethal Obsession

An Enemies to Lovers Romantic Thriller

Amanda Shittim

Bridgewater & Buchner
Publishing Co.

For all of us.

There is no friend as loyal as a book.

— Ernest Hemmingway

PROLOGUE: THE BETRAYAL

Lena

Numbers run like little electric men, marching in endless lines. Too many. Never enough. They blur, swimming past as if they can escape the green-eyed beast hunting them. I don't blink, won't stop.

I've cracked bigger puzzles, forced patterns from chaos, exposed truths even the liars didn't know.

This one—this one is close, and it has Dante's name scrawled all over it. One more piece, and I've got him. Then the universe coughs up an unexpected punch line: glass shatters, and a bullet whizzes by my head.

WTF!

My brain goes into overdrive. Breath stalls as glass explodes around me, a kaleidoscope of destruction that does not include death today, thank you very much. My hand slams on the keyboard, and I'm already moving, chair spinning away like it never wanted me to sit there in the first place.

Cold night air rushes through the shattered window, a rude reminder that I'm alive.

The laptop is a million dollars, and several other people's problems are compressed into one expensive aluminum shell. I clutch it like the Holy Grail as my heels strike the floor, sharp and fast. Fuck. It could've been my head. A clean hole where a bullet met a skull, it had no business getting to know. My mouth tastes like adrenaline, and I smell panic in the air. It's me.

One breath. Two. I'm not dead. Everything else is manageable.

The penthouse door looms ahead, and I swear I can feel Dante's eyes on me, those fucking artic-blue orbs always calculating. Is he watching me now? I make it out to the hallway, darkness swallowing me up like a crime scene body bag.

My heart tries to punch its way out of my chest. I lean against the wall, breathing hard, letting my brain catch up with my instincts.

Alive. I've got that going for me. But for how long?

GHOSTS OF LAST NIGHT'S RAIN LINGER LIKE drunks, slumped in every gutter and alley. The streets are slick with regrets, shining with lies reflected from the awakening skyline.

At this hour, the city's pulse is slow, a sleeping beast unaware of the predator in its midst. Me.

I move through the shadows, driven by an urgency that overpowers everything else, even the raw edges of my nerves. There's no room for fear, only the cold, hard search for answers.

I push forward, dodging doubts like bullets, leaving a trail that leads straight to Dante Voss.

Each step fuels the fire, a controlled burn that keeps me moving past shuttered storefronts and empty intersections.

My heels splash through reflective puddles, each one a mirror to the steel and glass world Dante's built for himself.

He thinks he's untouchable, the king of a kingdom where nothing can challenge his throne. I'm about to topple his world, but first I have to get there.

The echo of whispers and clinking glasses suddenly fills my head, a flashback with claws. The charity gala. A night I can't afford to forget. A room packed with people in black-tie armor, all watching each other as closely as they watch the auction block.

I remember the dress I wore—scarlet and calculated to make a statement. It had been a battle of glances and wine-fueled promises. Dante had found me there, his gaze an invitation and a challenge. We never talked, not with words. But he'd seen me. And I'd seen him.

The memory kicks me forward as I reach Voss Security's looming entrance. Glass and steel, as impenetrable as Dante's own expression. Early employees shuffle past, eyes flicking to me in something between shock and recognition.

The woman who died last night, standing here like a damn ghost. My hair's pulled tight and severe, heels a percussion line that echoes my insistence.

I shove through the revolving doors, each turn pulling me deeper into his lair. The lobby's all sharp lines and cold surfaces, screaming money and power. My pulse keeps time with the tick of expensive clocks.

The clocks say I'm already too late, but fuck them. I don't plan on listening to anything but the beating of my own war drum.

Long corridors stretch out before me, more mirror than marble. I see myself in every surface, a thousand reflections, none of them sure. My steps falter, but only for a second.

Keep going, Lena. One foot in front of the other. I think of the bullet, the shattered glass, the close call that feels even closer with each echoing stride. How much does he know? How much did he want to know?

I don't stop until I reach Dante's office door. My hand raises to knock, trembling, but not from fear. The words slip out, defiant, an answer to a question he hasn't asked yet.

"We need to talk, Dante."

I see my reflection again, this time in the glass that surrounds me, framing my face like a picture.

Like a warning, I take a breath and get ready to meet my traitor.

THE ENEMY'S DEN

Lena

I throw open the door to Dante's office, a bastion of mahogany and control, my eyes locking with his as I fling the folder across his desk. Papers fly like startled birds.

"What the fuck is this?" I demand, my voice echoing like a shot. But before I can get an answer, chaos erupts—a splintering crash, distant shouts. The building's under attack.

An avalanche of mahogany and white sheets spills across the desk as the folder lands between us, and the papers fall like accusations. Dante stares, a glacier with artic-blue eyes now turning to steel. He wasn't expecting me. Damn right he wasn't. I didn't bother making an appointment. My heart is racing, and I've barely started.

He looks from the mess on his desk to my eyes, his surprise quickly smoothed over with a chilling calm. I'm the hurricane to his iceberg. "Lena," he says, like a curse or a prayer. I can't tell which.

I stand my ground, shoulders squared and fury thrumming beneath my skin. I'm ready for a fight.

"You lied to me," I spit, and the words cut the air like knives.

He arches an eyebrow, all cool indifference, but there's something darker flickering beneath. "I don't know what you're talking about."

"I followed the money."

He straightens, his posture rigid as the suit of armor he's wearing. His silence speaks volumes, but I'm not backing down. I've come too far for that.

"Why?" I push, needing the answer like a drowning woman needs air. My eyes are locked onto his, and the tension crackles between us, alive and hungry. It's a dangerous tango we're dancing, but I refuse to follow his lead.

And then the world explodes. The sharp crack of breaking glass, shouting voices, the chaos a sudden, roaring storm. We're under attack, and my instincts shift in an instant from demanding answers to surviving the next second.

"Down!" Dante's voice cuts through the noise, all command and urgency. He's on the move, fast and precise, crossing the room to me as debris flies and glass rains down like deadly confetti.

The door bursts open, and two men barrel through, their eyes wild and guns drawn. I freeze for a heartbeat, too short to die but long enough to feel the rush of adrenaline firing through my veins.

One of them shouts something, but the words are lost in the clamor. A shot echoes, and a picture frame shatters behind me. I dive behind the desk, my laptop clattering to the floor, my heart pounding in my ears like war drums.

Dante is beside me in a flash, the eye of the storm, calm and dangerous. The two gunmen advance, but I see it in Dante's eyes—he's already calculating, already five steps ahead.

"Lena," he says, low and steady, his eyes locked on mine. It's not a question. It's a promise.

The air buzzes with urgency and panic, alarms shrieking, the walls vibrating with the force of it all. He reaches for my hand, and in that charged second, it's like nothing else matters.

I grab his wrist instead, my grip as fierce as his. We're on our feet, moving, driven by the need to stay alive. Another shot, the sound splitting the air like a scream, but I'm running, Dante pulling me behind him, every step a heartbeat, every heartbeat a countdown.

The corridor is chaos, red lights flashing, casting bloody shadows over everything. Staff scramble for cover, the orderly corporate world thrown into frantic disarray. I barely register the faces, the fear, the scattered debris—we're moving too fast, and all I can focus on is escape.

Dante leads me down a side hallway, concrete and industrial, a stark contrast to the polished glass above. It's dark, cavernous, my pulse echoing off the walls as the emergency lights strobe like a dying heartbeat.

Behind us, the clamor fades, but not enough to be safe. Not nearly enough. I catch a glimpse of movement, a shadow that means we're still hunted, still targets. We don't stop. We don't look back.

He hauls open a metal door, and I don't hesitate. I'm through it, into the blinding brightness of the street, the rush of the city a sudden, jarring contrast to the chaos inside.

An armored car is waiting, sleek and ready. The driver's-side window slides down as we approach, and I see a flash of salt and pepper hair, a glimpse of the one person I think I can trust.

"Get in," Marcus says, his voice smooth and urgent, Dante's right-hand man. He gestures for us to hurry, but I know better. This isn't a rescue. It's a trap.

My mind races, calculating, and I'm about to pull back when Dante makes the decision for us. He shoves me inside, covering me with his weight, his strength leaving no room for argument.

We're in, the doors slamming shut with a finality that feels like the end of everything. Marcus throws a smirk over his shoulder as the engine roars to life, the city blurring past the windows.

I'm too shocked, too furious, to care. We're alive, but I don't know for how long.

THE STREET IS A BLUR OF NOISE AND LIGHT, THE street a dizzying rush of lights and speed. My pulse is wild, matching the insane velocity of our escape. My brain struggles to catch up, to make sense of the chaos.

"Dante, they're still coming," Marcus says, his tone infuriatingly composed. He swerves, narrowly missing a truck, and I can almost hear the smile in his voice. The smile of a man who thinks he's won.

Dante's weight lifts off me, and I sit up, anger and adrenaline mixing in a potent cocktail. "He knew," I say, the accusation a spear aimed at both of them. Marcus, the untouchable bastard, and Dante, the fool who might believe him.

Dante's silence is its own kind of violence. His eyes burn, and I wonder if it's at Marcus, at the world, or at me for not trusting him. We've left the gunmen behind, but not the danger, not the lies.

Marcus navigates the car like a conductor leading a symphony of chaos, the city blurring by in neon streaks. I watch him, this man who's played us all, and feel the familiar weight of betrayal. Heavy and suffocating, like the end of everything.

"You can't outrun them," Dante says, his voice tight as he fixes his gaze ahead, the skyline a jagged horizon of broken trust and shattered plans.

Marcus shifts gears, the car surging forward. "That's why I picked you up," he replies, his tone smooth and calculating. "Teamwork, remember?"

I laugh, the sound bitter and sharp. I can't help it. It's absurd, this deadly game he's playing. Absurd and terrifying and almost, almost thrilling.

But there's no room for thrill when the stakes are this high. No room for anything except the raw, consuming need to survive and the cold determination to make it out alive.

I don't know where we're going or who will be left standing when we get there. All I know is the furious beat of my heart, and the man sitting next to me might be the only two things I can't afford to lose.

THE GILDED CAGE

Lena
    The iron gates slam shut behind me, and the sound feels like a lock clicking into place. Trapped. I force my breathing to stay even, but my pulse is a traitor, hammering in my ears as I take in the sprawling estate before me. It's too much. Too luxurious. Too calculated.

A fortress disguised as a home. A prison dressed in gold.

Dante strides ahead, his presence a storm at my side, powerful and inescapable. My mind races, trying to untangle the truth from the lies. The missing money. The attacks. The impossible coincidence of him being at the center of it all. I should be grateful for his so-called protection, but I can't shake the feeling that I've walked straight into the lion's den.

Every instinct screams at me to run. But where?

Instead, I steel my spine and keep my distance, scanning for exits, for weaknesses. For the moment he proves me right.

. . .

Dante

She hesitates. I can feel the weight of her suspicion pressing against me like a blade at my throat. She doesn't trust me.

That shouldn't bother me.

It does.

Lena moves like a caged animal, her sharp eyes tracking every detail, cataloging threats I would never allow to reach her. The idea that she sees me as one of them—one of the threats—grates under my skin. I've built this estate to withstand enemies, to keep danger out. And yet, she looks at me like I'm the one locking her in.

Damn frustrating woman.

I lengthen my stride, needing space, needing control. But she doesn't let up.

"You really expect me to believe this is for my protection?" Her voice is sharp, cutting. "Or just your way of keeping me where you want me?"

I stop. Turn to face her.

The tension between us snaps tight. Her chin is raised, defiant, but her fingers tremble at her sides. She's afraid. I hate that. I hate that I might be the reason.

"You think I need to trap you, Lena?" My voice drops low, measured. "You're free to leave. But if you walk out that gate, I can't guarantee you'll make it through the night."

Her breath catches. Just for a second. But I catch it.

Lena

I hate that he might be right.

I hate that I even hesitate.

But I've seen the bodies. I've felt the bullets slicing too close. And I still don't know *who* is pulling the strings. The smart move is staying inside, staying close, using him as a shield until I can untangle the truth.

Still, the way he watches me—like I'm some puzzle he's trying to solve—sends a shiver down my spine.

I force myself to scoff. "Right. Because being in *here* with you is so much safer."

His jaw ticks, and for a second, I think I've won. But then he steps closer, crowding my space without touching me. His scent—something dark, woody, and expensive—wraps around me, and I have to fight not to react.

"You don't have to like me," he murmurs. "You just have to stay alive."

The worst part?

I don't know which option terrifies me more.

Dante

She doesn't flinch. I respect that.

I shouldn't admire the fire in her, the way she refuses to be cowed, but damn if it doesn't make me want to push her just to see how much she can take. She doesn't trust me. I don't blame her. But that doesn't mean I'm letting her walk into a death sentence just because she's too stubborn to see the truth.

Then the alarms blare.

I don't hesitate. My hand wraps around her wrist, yanking her toward me as I reach for my gun with the other.

Her gasp is sharp, but she doesn't pull away. She's already scanning the space, her mind working, calculating.

Good.

Because this isn't just about me protecting her anymore.

It's about surviving. Together.

LENA

Adrenaline surges through me as Dante pulls me behind cover. My heart pounds—not just from the danger but from the way our bodies press together in the chaos. The estate is supposed to be impenetrable. *So how the hell is someone inside?*

I barely have time to process before Dante moves. He's efficient, controlled, issuing orders into his earpiece while keeping me close. It's infuriating that he's this composed while my brain is a hurricane of questions and worst-case scenarios.

And then—silence.

A pause, stretching between heartbeats.

I turn my head just as he does. Our faces inches apart. Breathing hard. Alive.

His eyes drop to my lips.

And suddenly, I don't know if the pounding in my chest is fear or something far more dangerous.

Dante

I should move.

I don't.

Her breath is warm against my skin, her lips parted, her pulse fluttering at her throat. I tell myself this is just adrenaline, that this tension crackling between us is nothing more than survival instincts on overdrive.

Lying to myself has never been my strong suit.

Before I can think better of it, I close the distance.

Her breath hitches, but she doesn't pull away. The second my mouth claims hers, it's fire—hot, urgent, laced with everything we don't have time to admit.

And then, just as fast as it started, she shoves me back.

We stare at each other, wide-eyed, breathing heavy.

Lena

What the hell just happened?

I wipe the back of my hand across my mouth as if I can erase the heat, the taste of him still lingering. My body is betraying me, every nerve alive, wanting more. *No. No, no, no.*

This was a mistake.

Dante's expression darkens, his jaw tight, as if he's just realized the same thing.

He steps back. "Go inside."

I don't argue. I don't look back.

But as I walk away, my mind is a battlefield. Between logic and something far more dangerous.

I need the truth.

I *can't* want him.

And yet, the ghost of his kiss lingers, setting fire to my resolve.

I STORM THROUGH THE CORRIDORS OF DANTE'S estate, each step too loud, too fast, fueled by frustration and something far more dangerous. My lips still tingle from the kiss—a mistake, a moment of weakness. My mind screams at me to erase it, to pretend it never happened.

But my body remembers.

Damn him.

I reach the nearest guest suite, pushing the heavy wooden door open and slamming it shut behind me. The room is just as extravagant as the rest of this place—vaulted ceilings, silk drapes, a massive bed that looks entirely too inviting. I ignore all of it, pacing like a caged animal.

My fingers brush my lips before I catch myself. *No.*

I need to focus.

The attack wasn't random. Someone got past Dante's security—his *impenetrable* security—which means there's a leak, or worse, the enemy is more powerful than we thought.

I move to the window, parting the curtain just enough to glimpse the estate's perimeter. The guards are already tightening security, sweeping the grounds. I spot Dante below, barking orders, his body tense, movements sharp with barely contained fury.

He kissed me.

I kissed him back.

I groan, pressing my forehead against the cool glass. This can't happen. Not with him. Not when I still don't know if he's the mastermind behind all of this or just another piece in a much larger game.

I need to be smart.

I need to get to the truth.

And I need to stay the hell away from Dante Voss.

Dante

I watch her retreat, every muscle in my body locked tight with frustration.

That kiss—Jesus. It was supposed to be nothing. A byproduct of adrenaline, of proximity. But the second my lips met hers, I knew it was more. And now she's running.

Fine. Let her.

I have bigger problems right now.

I turn back to Marco, my head of security, who's waiting with a grim expression. "Tell me."

"The breach was internal," he says, keeping his voice low. "Whoever got in had access to the estate's security codes. This wasn't a mistake—it was sabotage."

My jaw tightens. I expected as much, but hearing it confirmed sends a slow, burning fury through me.

"How many men did we lose?"

"Two. Both outside perimeter guards." Marco exhales, glancing toward the west wall. "Whoever they were, they weren't here to kill you outright. They were looking for something. Or *someone*."

My stomach knots.

Lena.

I already suspected she was the target, but this seals it. Someone wants her dead, and they're willing to come onto *my* territory to make it happen. That's a level of boldness I don't tolerate.

She's not safe here.

She's not safe anywhere.

And now, with the way my body still hums from that damn kiss, the stakes feel even higher.

I run a hand through my hair, forcing my voice into something calmer. "Double the patrols. No one gets in or out without my say-so."

Marco nods, hesitating for a beat. "And Lena?"

I glance up toward her window. The curtains are drawn now, blocking any view inside.

"She stays," I say, my voice firm. "Whether she likes it or not."

LENA

I don't sleep.

I sit at the desk in the guest suite, my laptop open, fingers scrolling through financial records—proof that something is very, *very* wrong.

The discrepancies I found before were just the beginning. Millions of dollars unaccounted for. Transfers rerouted through shell companies. And now, the deeper I dig, the clearer the picture becomes.

This isn't just theft.

It's a setup.

And the more I connect the dots, the more I realize that the man I should be most afraid of might not be Dante after all.

I rub my temples, exhaustion tugging at me, but I don't stop. I can't. I need to know *who* is behind this, and why they want me dead.

A knock at the door makes me jolt.

I hesitate. Then, "What?"

Dante's voice is low. "Open the door, Lena."

I should ignore him.

But I don't.

I move to the door, unlocking it, but I don't step back. He fills the doorway, dark and imposing, his expression unreadable.

"We need to talk," he says.

I cross my arms. "About how you let assassins waltz onto your estate?"

His eyes narrow. "About how someone *inside* my estate let them in."

That gives me pause.

"What are you saying?"

He exhales, stepping inside without invitation. His presence changes the air—too close, too consuming. I force myself to hold my ground.

"I'm saying we have a traitor." His gaze locks onto mine, sharp and knowing. "And I think you know more than you're telling me."

I stiffen. "Excuse me?"

He leans in, his voice a near growl. "I've seen you working. You think I haven't noticed the way you've been digging into things? You don't trust me, fine. But don't insult me by pretending you're just a victim in this."

I swallow hard. *Damn him.*

I could lie. Pretend I don't know what he's talking about.

Or I could do something far more dangerous— tell him the truth.

Dante

She doesn't answer right away.

Instead, she searches my face, like she's weighing something, deciding just how much to give away.

Then, finally—

"I found something," she says, voice quieter now. "A financial trail. Money moving in ways it shouldn't. And I think..." She hesitates, then takes a breath. "I think someone's setting you up, Dante."

I go still.

Because I expected her to tell me something. I expected accusations, half-truths.

But not this.

"Explain," I demand.

She steps back to her laptop, turning the screen toward me. Numbers, bank accounts, transactions—I recognize the names. *Shit*.

She keeps going. "At first, I thought *you* were the one laundering money. But now? This isn't just embezzlement. It's a frame job. Someone wants it to look like you're dirty. And they've been planning this for a long time."

I process her words, my mind clicking through possibilities, enemies. There are too many. And yet, if what she's saying is true—if someone is orchestrating this from the shadows—then we're dealing with more than just a financial crime.

This is personal.

And Lena is at the center of it.

I step closer, my voice dropping. "Do you realize what this means?"

She nods, swallowing. "It means the people after me aren't just trying to kill me." Her voice wavers, just slightly. "They're trying to destroy *you* too."

For a moment, neither of us speaks.

The weight of it settles between us.

Then I make a decision.

"You're not going anywhere," I tell her. "You and I? We're in this together now."

Her lips part like she wants to argue. But she doesn't.

Because deep down, she knows it too.

The only way we survive this?

Is if we stop fighting each other—and start fighting the real enemy.

A DANGEROUS GAME

L **ena**

I can still taste him.

Even as I pace the length of my room, arms crossed, mind racing—I can still feel the phantom press of Dante's lips against mine, the heat of his body caging me in, the hunger in his kiss that stole my breath.

It was a mistake. A moment of weakness.

And yet, my pulse betrays me, humming with the memory.

I shake my head, inhaling deeply. *Focus, Lena. Focus.*

Dante might be the only thing standing between me and a bullet, but that doesn't mean I trust him. His entire life is built on secrets, on power plays I can barely begin to untangle. And the longer I stay under his roof, the more tangled *I* become in his world.

I glance at my laptop, still open on the desk where I left it. The financial discrepancies aren't just a coincidence—someone is setting both of us up. I was right to suspect him before, but now I'm starting to think he's as much a pawn in this as I am.

But I need proof.

Slipping quietly toward the door, I press my ear against it. The estate is silent, thick walls swallowing sound, but I know better than to assume I'm unwatched. Dante doesn't strike me as a man who leaves things to chance.

I reach for the handle. Just a quick look. A few minutes to dig into his office, maybe find something he wouldn't willingly tell me.

I twist the knob and step out into the long corridor.

But the second I shut the door behind me—A hand slams against the door above my head.

DANTE

I knew she'd try something.

Lena might be smart, but she's predictable when cornered—always looking for a way out, always ready to run. That's why I stationed myself outside her door, arms crossed, waiting.

And now, as she tries to slip away, I move before she even has a chance to react.

My palm flattens against the door, trapping her in place. She sucks in a sharp breath, and when she turns, her eyes blaze with defiance.

I should step back.

I don't.

"What exactly are you doing?" My voice is low, even, but she knows better than to mistake it for patience.

Lena tilts her chin up. "Taking a walk."

I smirk. "Try again."

She presses her back against the door, trying to create space between us, but I don't give her any.

My body heat radiates between us, the air thick with something more dangerous than anger.

She swallows, her throat bobbing. "Move."

I drag my gaze over her, taking in the way her pulse jumps at the base of her throat. "Not until you tell me where you were planning to go."

Her lips part, hesitation flickering across her face. She's good at lying—I'll give her that—but I know what she's after.

"You were going to my office."

Lena exhales sharply, eyes narrowing. "If you already know, why ask?"

I lean in, close enough to catch the scent of her —something warm and intoxicating beneath the stubborn front she wears like armor. "Because I want to hear you admit it."

Her jaw tightens. "You're an arrogant ass."

I grin. "And you're a terrible liar."

She tries to push past me, but I catch her wrist, pulling her flush against me. Her breath hitches— just for a second. But I catch it.

Electricity snaps between us, sharp and undeniable.

She glares up at me. "Let. Me. Go."

I should.

Instead, I reach down, brush my fingers along the pulse at her wrist. It's racing. Not with fear— something else.

Something I *want* to push.

"You want to search my office?" My voice is low, a murmur against her skin. "Go ahead. I'll even escort you. But don't pretend you're not playing a dangerous game, Lena."

Her breath shudders, her fingers curling against

my chest. For a fraction of a second, I wonder if she'll push me away—or pull me closer.

Then she wrenches free.

"Stay the hell out of my way, Dante."

She storms off, disappearing back into her room, slamming the door.

I exhale slowly, running a hand through my hair.

That woman is going to be the death of me.

Lena

I can't sleep.

Even with the heavy curtains drawn, the room shrouded in darkness, my body refuses to relax. Every time I close my eyes, I see him—his smirk, the way his grip burned against my wrist, the way his voice curled around my name like a whispered promise.

I groan, flipping onto my stomach.

I need to get out of here.

Not just this room. *This house. This world.*

Because if I stay any longer, I might forget why I came here in the first place.

I might forget that the real danger isn't just the men hunting me in the shadows.

It's the one standing right in front of me.

Dante

I don't sleep.

Instead, I sit in my office, staring at the financial records Lena unearthed.

She's right.

Someone is orchestrating this—manipulating

numbers, redirecting money in a way that's too deliberate to be random. Someone wants me to take the fall.

And they want her dead.

I lean back in my chair, exhaling slowly. The weight of the night presses against me, the scent of her still clinging to my skin.

I should be focused on the numbers, the betrayal lurking beneath them.

But all I can think about is the way Lena looked at me in that hallway—like she hated how much she wanted me.

Like she wanted me to lose control.

I smirk, shaking my head.

She's playing with fire.

But so am I.

LENA

I wake up in a haze of heat.

Dante's hands—trailing fire across my skin. His lips—brushing my throat, teasing, tasting.

My body reacts before my mind fully registers that it's not real.

It's a dream.

I jolt upright, heart slamming against my ribs, breath coming in sharp, uneven gasps.

The room is quiet, the air still.

But my body burns.

I shove the covers off, pacing to the window, pressing my palms against the cool glass. *Get a grip, Lena.*

I will *not* let him get under my skin.

I will *not* let a kiss—a mistake—turn into some-thing I *want*.

I press my forehead against the glass, inhaling deep, trying to steady myself.

But even as I do, I know the truth.

The real danger isn't just out there, lurking in the shadows.

It's here.

It's *him*.

DANTE

The sun hasn't risen yet, but I don't need sleep.

I sit in my office, fingers steepled beneath my chin, watching security footage. The breach last night—too clean. Too precise.

An inside job.

I should be focused on finding the traitor. On eliminating the threat before they make another move.

But my thoughts keep drifting—to her.

Lena.

The way she looked at me when I pinned her against that door. The way her body trembled—not with fear, but something darker, something she doesn't want to admit.

She's still fighting me.

Still fighting herself.

I smirk.

For now.

Because one way or another—whether she likes it or not—she and I are in this together.

And I *never* lose.

THE ENEMY INSIDE

Lena

The remnants of my dream cling to me as dawn creeps through the heavy curtains. I wake with my skin burning, my breath uneven, the phantom sensation of Dante's touch still whispering across my body.

It was just a dream.

But my body doesn't seem to care.

I roll onto my back, staring at the ceiling, trying to will away the images that flicker in my mind—his hands gripping my hips, his mouth trailing heat down my throat.

I groan, pressing my palms over my eyes. *Get it together, Lena.*

This isn't about him.

I push myself out of bed, shaking off the remnants of sleep and lust. The kiss, the tension, all of it —it's a distraction. I need to remember why I'm here. Why I *can't* let myself get lost in Dante's orbit.

And I have work to do.

Slipping on a silk guest robe over my guest pajamas reminds me of the absurdity of my circumstances. My enemy, bodyguard, protector, and host has thought of everything. I pad barefoot across the room to my laptop. Dante thinks he has me under lock and key, but I've hacked my way into systems far more secure than his.

It's time to find the truth.

DANTE

I can't focus.

Not on the breach, not on the financial discrepancies—hell, not even on the traitor lurking in my own damn estate.

All I can think about is *her*.

Lena.

Her sharp mind, her stubborn fire, the way her body fit against mine last night like she was made to be there.

I exhale, running a hand through my hair, trying to force my thoughts into submission. This isn't me. I don't get *distracted*. I don't let my control slip.

But when it comes to Lena?

My usual rules don't seem to apply.

I stand at my office window, watching the estate grounds come to life with the first light of morning. Security teams move through their rotations, reinforcing every possible weakness after last night's intrusion. But my instincts tell me that the real threat isn't outside these walls.

It's inside.

And if I'm right, Lena might be in more danger than either of us realized.

· · ·

LENA

I slip into Dante's system with ease, bypassing firewalls like they were made of paper. He might be powerful, but he's underestimated me.

The data sprawls before me—bank transactions, encrypted messages, surveillance feeds. I scroll through them, searching for inconsistencies, for something that ties this all together.

And then I see it.

A name. A familiar transaction. A forged signature.

Dante isn't the one laundering money.

He's being framed.

The realization slams into me, my breath catching.

I was so convinced he was the enemy. That he was the one playing me. But this... this changes everything.

Before I can process it fully, the estate alarms explode into the air, a blaring siren that rattles my bones.

The estate has been breached.

DANTE

The second the alarms sound, I move.

I grab my gun, shoving through my office doors, instincts on high alert. I reach Lena's room in seconds, my pulse a steady, controlled rhythm despite the chaos.

I don't knock. I *don't* wait.

I burst through the door to find her in front of her laptop, eyes wide, fingers frozen over the keyboard.

She was searching.

Dammit, Lena.

But now isn't the time.

"Move." My voice is sharp, brooking no argument. "We need to get out of here."

She hesitates, only for a second, but it's enough to make me grit my teeth.

"Dante—"

"No time."

I grab her wrist, pulling her to her feet just as gunfire shatters the air.

She gasps, her body instinctively pressing into mine. I shift, shielding her, scanning the hall outside.

Someone's inside.

And they're coming straight for us.

Lena

I don't fight Dante's grip. Not when the sound of bullets ripping through the walls makes my blood run cold.

This is real. *Too real.*

His body is solid against mine, his heat grounding me even as my mind races. We move together, instinctively in sync, slipping into the shadows of the hallway.

The house is too quiet now, the alarms still wailing but no guards in sight. That's what scares me the most.

"Where the hell are your men?" I whisper.

Dante's jaw is tight, his expression unreadable. "Taken out or compromised."

My stomach clenches. If the breach was planned, it means whoever's inside *knows* this house.

And they want us dead.

We reach a back stairwell, Dante leading the way with practiced efficiency, his gun steady in his grip.

"Stay close," he orders.

I don't argue.

Because for once, I *want* to be close.

DANTE

I hear them before I see them.

Footsteps—controlled, calculated. Not amateurs. Professionals.

I press Lena into the wall, my body a shield between her and the danger. Her breath is warm against my neck, her hands gripping my shirt.

"You armed?" I murmur.

Her lips brush my ear as she whispers back. "Took my gun. Yours is all we've got."

I swear under my breath. *Who the hell disarmed her?*

The footsteps get closer.

We don't have time.

I turn my head slightly, catching her gaze. "We need a distraction."

Her brows furrow. "Like what?"

I don't answer.

I just do it.

I grab her by the waist, yanking her flush against me. Her gasp is swallowed as my mouth crashes onto hers, heat exploding between us.

For a second, she freezes.

Then she *melts*.

Her hands fist in my shirt, her body arching into mine as I deepen the kiss, pouring every ounce of urgency, of hunger, into it.

And just like that, the air between us *ignites*.

Lena

I don't think. I can't.

Not when Dante's hands are gripping my hips, pulling me against him like he *owns* me.

Not when his tongue slides against mine, his body heat drowning me, his scent wrapping around me like a vice.

My mind screams at me to push him away.

My body betrays me, pressing closer, *wanting*.

The footsteps pause outside the stairwell.

Then, voices. Confused.

They think we're just lovers caught in the wrong place.

It's working.

But this—*this*—is no longer pretend.

When Dante's lips leave mine, my breath shudders, my pulse a riot beneath my skin.

His eyes are dark, burning with something raw and *dangerous*.

We stare at each other, still tangled, the world around us momentarily forgotten.

And then—

Gunfire.

The moment shatters.

Dante

I don't hesitate.

I grab Lena, yanking her behind cover as bullets tear through the stairwell.

I fire back, taking down one of the intruders, but there are more.

Too many.

"Lena, go." My voice is sharp, commanding.

She doesn't move.

I glance at her, expecting defiance—but what I see instead is something sharper.

Determination.

She looks at me like she's made a decision.

Like she *trusts* me.

My chest tightens.

Another round of gunfire.

We move together, side by side.

Whether we like it or not—we're in this together now.

THE DUST SETTLES. THE INTRUDERS RETREAT, but the message is clear.

This isn't just an attack.

It's a warning.

Lena

My body still burns—from adrenaline, from the fight, from *him*.

I should be thinking about the enemy we just faced. The deeper conspiracy I've just uncovered.

But all I can think about is the way Dante kissed me.

The way I *let* him.

The way I *wanted* him.

I wrap my arms around myself, trying to steady my breath, my thoughts.

This is dangerous.
Not just the people hunting us.
But *him*.
Because if I'm not careful...
I might not want to run anymore.

BREAKING POINT

L**ena**
    The so-called safe house is nothing like Dante's estate. No gilded halls, no sprawling luxury—just a dimly lit space tucked away in the outskirts of the city. Sparse furniture, reinforced walls, and a lingering scent of gun oil. A place meant for survival, not comfort.

It should make me feel safer.

It doesn't.

Because Dante is here.

And *he* is the real danger.

I sit on the edge of the small bed, staring at the floor, my body still wired from the last twenty-four hours. I'm grateful that one of Dante's men, Marco, got me a change of clothes. I shed the silk ensemble with a matching robe for a pair of jeans, a t-shirt, and sneakers; I don't know how Dante' knew my size or where he just happened to have a pair of women's sneakers lying around that fit me perfectly, but again Dante's thought of everything. Everything. The attack, the betrayal, the way Dante shielded me with his own body—*the way he kissed me.*

I exhale shakily, rubbing my hands over my arms. I can't afford to get distracted. Can't afford to let the way his touch set me on fire take root in my mind.

But when the door clicks shut and I glance up, Dante is watching me.

And suddenly, the air is too thick.

Dante

I should walk away.

I should put distance between us, focus on the threats still lurking in the shadows.

But I don't.

Instead, I take a step closer, drawn to the way Lena's breath catches, the way her fingers tighten against the fabric of her jeans.

She's afraid.

Not of me.

Of *this*.

Of *us*.

"We need to talk," I say, my voice low.

She exhales, shaking her head. "No, we don't."

I smirk. "Lena—"

"No." She stands abruptly, backing up until she hits the wall. Her chin lifts in defiance, but I can see the truth in her eyes.

She wants to fight this. *Wants* to pretend it doesn't exist.

But we both know better.

I move closer, closing the distance between us until there's nothing left but heat and tension. My hands brace against the wall beside her head, caging her in without touching her.

Her breath shudders.

"What are you doing?" she whispers.

"Something I should've done the second I met you," I murmur.

And then, I kiss her.

LENA

The second his lips claim mine, I shatter.

I don't think. I don't *want* to think.

Because the moment I let myself feel, there's no going back.

Dante kisses me like he's trying to consume me, like he's been starving for this just as much as I have. My hands slide into his hair, tugging him closer, needing *more*.

He groans, deep and rough, before lifting me effortlessly. My legs wrap around his waist as he carries me to the bed, never breaking the kiss.

I know this is dangerous.

I know this changes *everything*.

But right now, I don't care.

Because for the first time in a long time—maybe ever—I *want* to fall.

DANTE

Lena is fire in my hands.

I've wanted this—*her*—from the moment I saw her at the gala, from the moment she stormed into my office with that sharp tongue and fearless gaze. But this? This is more than want.

This is need.

Her nails rake down my back as I lay her against the bare sheets, her body arching beneath mine. I take my time, savoring every gasp, every shudder, memorizing the way she melts for me.

She's responsive, her body arching into my touch, her hands gripping the sheets. I can feel her desire building, her need mirroring my own.

I move lower, my lips brushing her stomach through her t-shirt, my hands sliding up her thighs. She's trembling, her breath coming in short gasps, and I pause, just for a moment, to drink in the sight of her. Her jeans hug her curves like a second skin, but they're a barrier I'm determined to remove. I quickly unbutton and unzip them, my fingers brushing the soft skin of her hips as I pull them down, inch by agonizing inch. She lifts her hips, desperate, and I savor her eagerness, my thumbs brushing the sensitive skin of her inner thighs.

"Dante," she pants, her voice thick with need, and I look up, meeting her eyes before dipping lower. Her clit is swollen, begging for attention, and I tease her, my tongue flicking lightly before sucking her into my mouth. She gasps, her hands tangling in my hair, her body bucking against me. I hum, the vibration sending shivers through her, and she moans, her legs falling open wider, giving me full access.

I take my time, lapping at her like she's the sweetest treat, my fingers sliding inside her, slick and tight around me. She's clenching, her walls fluttering as her orgasm builds, and I press deeper, fucking her with my fingers while my mouth works her clit.

"Fuck, Dante," she cries, her voice breaking as she comes apart, her juices flooding my mouth. I drink her in, devouring her like she's the only thing keeping me alive, and she shudders, her body trembling as she rides out her release.

But I'm not done. Not even close. I rise above her, my cock throbbing, aching to be inside her, and she reaches for me, her hands gripping my hips. I unzip my slacks, relieved for the chance to unleash the bulge growing inside. I tease her, pressing the head of my cock to her entrance, sliding it along her folds before pulling back, denying her. Her eyes flash with frustration, but her breath hitches, and I see the hunger in her gaze. This is our game now—tease and denial, power and surrender.

"Not yet," I murmur, my voice low and commanding. I lean down, kissing her neck, her collarbone, my lips trailing down to her breasts. Her shirt is still on, a barrier I'm in no rush to remove. I pull the fabric tight, trapping her nipples against the cotton, and she arches, a soft cry escaping her lips.

"Dante," she whimpers, her hands clawing at my shoulders.

I smile against her skin, a slow, dangerous curve of my lips. "Patience, Lena."

I sit back on my heels, taking in the sight of her. Her t-shirt is hiked-up halfway, her jeans pooled at her ankles, her panties discarded on the floor. She's a mess, and it's beautiful. I reach out, tracing the line of her thigh, my touch feather-light, deliberate. Her skin is warm and flushed, and I can see the goosebumps rise where my fingers pass.

She bites her lip, her eyes darkening with desire.

I chuckle, a low, rumbling sound.

I lean forward, pressing a kiss to the inside of her thigh, just where it meets her hip. She shivers, her breath catching, and I take my time, worshipping her skin with my lips, my tongue. I'm mapping her, memorizing every inch, every curve.

Her hands fist in the sheets, her body tense with anticipation. I can feel her need, a tangible thing, pulsing between us. I move closer, my breath ghosting over her core, but I don't touch her. Not yet. Instead, I trail my fingers up her stomach, teasing the edge of her t-shirt, pulling it tighter across her breasts.

"Dante," she groans, her voice a plea. "Now."

"No." My voice a whisper.

I press my palm to her stomach, feeling the rise and fall of her breath. She's trembling, her body on the edge, and I know I could push her over right now. But I don't. Instead, I pull back, sitting up, my eyes locking with hers.

"What do you want, Lena?" I ask, my voice steady, commanding.

She swallows, her chest heaving. "You. I want you."

I smile, a slow, dangerous curve of my lips. "Prove it."

Her eyes flash, a spark of defiance, but she nods, her hands reaching for me. I let her pull me closer, her fingers threading through my hair, her lips crashing against mine. It's hungry, desperate, and I let her take control, let her taste her own desire on my lips.

But I'm still in charge.

I break the kiss, pulling back slightly, my hands gripping her wrists. "Not so fast," I murmur, pressing her hands above her head, holding her in place. She struggles, just for a moment, before relaxing, her breath coming in short gasps.

"What are you doing?" she asks, her voice a mix of frustration and curiosity.

"Teaching you patience," I reply, my voice low. "And control."

I lean down, my lips brushing her ear, my breath hot against her skin. "You want me, Lena? Prove it. Show me how much you need me."

Her eyes close, her body arching into mine, and I feel her surrender, just a fraction. It's enough.

I release her wrists, my hands sliding down her arms, her sides, her thighs. She's trembling, her skin electric under my touch, and I take my time, worshipping her with my hands, my lips. I'm building the tension, layering it, until she's a taut string, ready to snap.

"Please," she whispers, her voice breaking. "Dante, I can't—"

"Shh," I murmur, pressing a finger to her lips. "Don't think. Just feel."

I lean down, my mouth capturing her nipple through her shirt, sucking hard, and she gasps, her body arching into me. I tease her, biting gently, pulling the fabric tight, and she moans, her hands fisting in my hair.

"Fuck, Dante," she groans. "I need—"

I pull back, my hands gripping her hips, holding her in place. "Not yet," I murmur, my voice a breathless command. "Not until I say so."

Her eyes flash with frustration, but she nods, her breath coming in short gasps. I can see the hunger in her gaze, the need, and it fuels me, pushes me to the edge.

I move lower, my lips trailing down her stomach, my hands sliding up her thighs. She's wet, so fucking wet, and I groan, my fingers brushing her core, teasing her, before pulling away. She doesn't know how long I've wanted this. I aim to make it last.

"Dante," she whimpers, her voice a plea. "Please."

I smile, a slow, dangerous curve of my lips. "Beg me."

Her eyes widen, just for a moment, then narrow. "Don't you do this. She shakes her head in a futile gesture of resistance. *But I got her.* She's too far gone. Please, Dante. I need this."

I lean down, pressing a kiss to her stomach, my hands sliding up her thighs, holding her open. "You need me," I murmur, my voice a whisper.

She bites her lip, her hands reaching for me, and I let her pull me closer, her fingers threading through my hair. She's trembling, her body on the edge, and I know I could push her over right now.

But I don't.

Instead, I pull back, sitting up, my eyes locking with hers. "What do you want, Lena?" I ask, my voice steady, commanding.

She swallows, her chest heaving. "You. I want you. Inside me. Now."

I smile, a slow, dangerous curve of my lips. "Say it again."

Her eyes flash, a spark of defiance, but she nods, her voice soft, desperate. "I want you, Dante. Inside me. Now."

I lean forward, pressing a kiss to her lips, my hands sliding down her body, teasing her, before pulling away. "Not yet," I murmur, my voice a command.

Her breath hitches, her body tense with anticipation, and I know I've got her right where I want her.

The room is heavy with tension, the air thick with the scent of her perfume, jasmine, and sandalwood, and the consistent odorous smell of gun oil mingling with the musk of her desire. I can feel her need, a tangible thing, pulsing between us, and I know this is just the beginning.

I rise, my body hovering above hers, my cock throbbing, aching to be inside her. But I don't move. Not yet. Instead, I lean down, my lips brushing her ear, my breath hot against her skin.

"You're mine, Lena," I murmur, my voice low, commanding. "Do you understand?"

I smile, a slow, dangerous curve of my lips.

And with that, I finally give in, pressing the head of my cock to her entrance, sliding it along her folds before pushing in slowly, inch by agonizing inch. She gasps, her eyes wide, her body stretching around me like a perfect fit.

"You feel so good," I groan, my voice rough, and I thrust deeper, burying myself fully.

She wraps her legs around me, her heels digging into my back as I begin to move, slow and deliberate at first, then harder, faster, our bodies slapping together. Her breasts heave with every thrust, I finally help her lift the t-shirt over her head, releasing her breasts, her nipples tight peaks, and I lean down, taking one into my mouth, sucking hard as I fuck her.

She's moaning my name, her voice a broken melody, and I lose myself in her, in the way she clenches around me, milking me, driving me closer to the edge.

But I'm not done. Not yet.

I pull back, my hands gripping her hips, holding her in place. "Not so fast," I murmur, my voice a command. "Where are you going?"

Her eyes flash with frustration and suspicion, her breath coming in short gasps. I can see the hunger in her gaze, the need, and it fuels me, pushes me to the edge. She would run if she could, but she can't. I got her right where I want her in more ways than one.

I chuckle. "I'm never letting you go, Lena."

I lean down, my lips capturing hers, my tongue dueling with hers as I thrust into her, slow and deliberate, each movement calculated, each touch deliberate.

"Dante," she whispers against my lips, her voice a plea, a demand.

"Ah. I—"

"Shh," I murmur, pressing a finger to her lips. "Don't think. Just feel."

And with that, I give in, snapping my hips faster, pounding into her with a primal urgency. Her walls tighten, her body convulsing as she comes again, screaming my name, and I follow, my orgasm ripping through me like a storm.

I spill into her, my seed hot and thick, my body trembling as I empty myself completely.

I collapse on top of her, my heart pounding, my breath ragged, and she wraps her arms around me, her legs still locked around my waist.

"Fuck," I whisper, pressing a kiss to her sweat-dampened skin, "You're everything I didn't know I needed."

Because after this, there's no going back.

I *won't* let her go.

LENA

When the dust settles, we lie tangled in the sheets, breathless and raw.

Dante's arm is draped over my waist, his fingers tracing slow, lazy circles on my hip. I should move. I Should put distance between us.

But I don't.

Because this isn't just heat.

It's something deeper.

And that terrifies me.

I turn my head slightly, meeting his gaze. "This complicates things."

He smirks, brushing his thumb across my lower lip. "They were already complicated."

I exhale, pressing my forehead against his chest.

We're falling.

And only heaven knows what we're in for next.

THE FINAL MOVE

L ena
The moment I wake up, I know something is wrong.

The sheets are cold beside me. Dante is gone.

A prickle of unease slithers down my spine as I sit up, rubbing the sleep from my eyes. The so-called safe house is silent—too silent. My instincts, honed from years of knowing when danger lurks just beneath the surface, scream at me to *move*. I quickly get my clothes on. Sneaks as well.

I reach for the gun Dante left on the nightstand.

But before I can even touch it, a hand clamps over my mouth.

I thrash, kicking, fighting, but my attacker is fast —*too* fast. A sharp pain stabs my neck, a needle piercing my skin.

The last thing I hear before darkness swallows me whole is a voice I recognize.

Marcus Chen.

DANTE

The second I step back into the safehouse and see the door ajar, my blood runs cold.

"Lena."

No answer.

A sickening dread claws at my chest as I storm inside, scanning the room. Sheets tangled. Her gun untouched. A struggle—but no signs of a body.

She's gone.

No. No. No.

I yank out my phone, dialing Marco. "Lena's been taken."

A curse on the other end. "We'll find her."

I already know *who* took her.

Marcus Chen.

My most trusted lieutenant. My *friend.*

Betrayal is a slow burn that turns to an inferno inside me.

And when I find him, I will burn him to the ground.

LENA

A throbbing pain pounds through my skull as I wake up, the taste of chemicals thick on my tongue. My limbs are heavy, sluggish, but my mind is sharp.

I'm tied to a chair. Hands bound.

I lift my head, blinking through the dim light.

Marcus stands a few feet away, arms crossed, watching me like I'm an animal in a cage.

"Rise and shine, princess," he says, smirking.

I take a slow, steady breath, forcing calm over my panic. "I should've known."

His smirk widens. "Yeah, you should have."

Bile rises in my throat, but I swallow it down. I need to *think.* Need to stall.

Because if I know one thing about Dante, it's that he's coming for me.

And when he does, *Marcus is a dead man.*

DANTE

I track them in under an hour.

Marcus is a cocky bastard—too confident in his ability to keep Lena hidden. He underestimated me.

My SUV screeches to a stop outside the abandoned warehouse. My men move into position, but I don't wait for backup.

This is personal.

This is *war.*

Gun drawn, I move fast, silent. The first guard goes down without a sound, my blade slipping between his ribs before he even registers I'm there.

By the time I reach the door, I already have blood on my hands.

And I'm just getting started.

LENA

Marcus paces in front of me, his monologue of self-righteous betrayal barely registering.

I'm too busy sawing through my bindings with the small blade I slipped from his own pocket.

Idiot.

He turns his back for a split second—just long enough for me to *move.*

I launch to my feet, the chair clattering to the ground. He barely has time to react before I slam my knee into his stomach.

He stumbles back, coughing. "You little—"

A gunshot echoes through the warehouse.

Not mine.

Not his.

Dante.

Dante

The second I see Lena standing, *free*, I don't hesitate.

I raise my gun and fire, hitting Marcus in the shoulder. He stumbles, rage twisting his features.

But it's not *me* he should be afraid of.

It's *her*.

Lena moves like lightning, grabbing the fallen gun, cocking it without a single moment of hesitation.

Marcus sees it too late.

She doesn't hesitate.

She doesn't flinch.

She pulls the trigger.

One shot. Right between the eyes.

It's over.

Lena

My hands tremble. My heart pounds.

Marcus crumples to the ground, blood pooling around his head.

I should feel something—regret, shock, *relief*.

But all I feel is *free*.

Dante steps toward me, his gaze dark, unreadable. "Are you okay?"

I nod, even though I'm not sure.

Then, before I can process it, he's pulling me

against him, his arms wrapping around me in a way that makes me feel *safe*.

I exhale, pressing my forehead to his chest. "It's over."

But he shakes his head. "Not yet."

Because now, we rebuild.

Together.

DANTE

Marcus was just the beginning.

There are more traitors. More threats. More shadows waiting to strike.

But Lena and I?

We're done running.

We work side by side, rooting out corruption in Voss Security, dismantling the web of deception Marcus left behind.

And through it all, Lena stays.

She fights beside me. Challenges me. *Trusts* me.

And I trust her.

That's the real victory.

Not just reclaiming my empire.

But earning *her*.

DANTE

Days bleed into nights, and still, Lena and I don't stop.

We dismantle every piece of Marcus's corruption, digging through years of carefully hidden betrayals, tracking down those who had their hands in my empire. Some of them beg. Some of them fight. None of them survive.

Lena is relentless.

I should be the one leading this charge, but she's right beside me, tireless, fearless, relentless.

I knew she was strong—I knew she was smart. But watching her now, watching her command respect in a world that would've swallowed most whole, I realize something else.

She was always meant for this.

And God help me, so was I.

Lena

I never imagined this would be my life.

Standing in the heart of Voss Security, sitting at the head of an empire I once thought was corrupt to its core. But the truth is, corruption doesn't come from power itself—it comes from the people who wield it.

And now, with Marcus gone, with the rot cut out at its source, Dante and I have the chance to do something different. Something better.

We don't just clean house—we *rebuild* it.

And through it all, Dante is there.

He watches me like I'm a mystery he's still trying to solve, like I'm a force he wasn't prepared for. And maybe he wasn't.

Neither was I.

Because the more time I spend beside him, the harder it is to pretend I don't *feel* something real.

Something dangerous.

Something I don't know if I'm ready for.

Dante

Trust is a rare thing in my world.

I've earned it from men who would die for me, from those who've bled beside me. But what I have with Lena?

It's different.

It's fragile, but unbreakable all at once.

She *challenges* me. Pushes me. Makes me better.

And now, as we sit in my office, staring at the finalized reports—Voss Security officially in the clear, Marcus's web of deception fully unraveled—I realize something else.

I don't want to do this without her.

I lean back in my chair, studying her from across the desk. She's focused, chewing on her bottom lip as she scans through the last of the financial reports, making sure nothing has slipped through the cracks.

She doesn't realize she does it—that little habit.

But I notice.

I notice *everything* about her.

And I'm done pretending I don't.

"We did it," I say, breaking the silence.

She exhales, setting the tablet down. "Yeah. We did."

But she doesn't look relieved.

She looks *conflicted*.

And I know why.

Because this was never just about fixing Voss Security.

It was about *us*.

About the fire burning between us, growing hotter by the day, by the hour, by the second.

And now that the fight is over, there's nothing left to hide behind.

No more excuses.

No more distractions.

Just us.

Lena

I can *feel* him watching me.

Dante Voss—*crime lord, business mogul, dangerous, infuriating man*—looking at me like I'm the only thing in this world that matters.

And damn it, I *hate* how much I like it.

This should be the part where I leave. Where I pack up, walk out, move on with my life like I always planned to.

But the thought of walking away makes my chest *ache*.

So I do what I do best.

I fight.

"You got what you wanted," I say, keeping my voice even. "Voss Security is yours again. Marcus is gone. The threat is neutralized."

Dante doesn't move, doesn't blink. "That's not all I want."

My pulse kicks up. "Dante—"

"You're still trying to run." His voice is calm, but there's steel beneath it. "Still trying to convince yourself you don't belong here."

I swallow. "I *don't* belong here."

He tilts his head, studying me like I'm some puzzle he's about to solve. "You *do* belong here, Lena. You always have."

His words send a tremor through me, sharp and unwelcome.

Because a part of me *wants* to believe him.

Wants to believe that I've found something here —something more than just survival.

Something *real*.

But real is dangerous.

Real is losing control.

And I've spent my whole life making sure I never *lose* control.

"I don't trust this," I whisper.

Dante stands, slow and deliberate. He walks around the desk, stopping just in front of me.

Close enough that I have to tilt my head to meet his gaze.

"Then trust *me*," he says softly.

And damn him—damn *me*—but I want to.

Because despite everything, despite the fear clawing at my chest, despite every reason I *should* walk away...

I can't.

I *won't*.

So instead of answering, instead of fighting—

I grab his collar, pull him down, and kiss him.

And this time, I don't *hold back*.

DANTE

She tastes like fire.

Like something I'll never get enough of.

Lena has fought me every step of the way, but this? *This* is her surrender.

Not in the way she thinks.

Not in weakness.

But in something stronger—*trust*.

I grip her waist, pulling her flush against me, deepening the kiss until there's no space between us, no hesitation.

She gasps against my mouth, hands fisting in my shirt, and I know.

I *know.*
She's mine.
And I'm hers.
There's no going back now.
And I don't want to.

LENA

When we finally break apart, I'm breathless.

Dante smirks down at me, his thumb tracing my jaw. "Still want to run?"

I exhale, resting my forehead against his chest.

And for the first time in a long, long time...

I don't.

EPILOGUE: OBSESSION

Dante

I find her exactly where I knew she'd be.

The sun has barely set, casting deep shadows along the city's skyline, but I don't need the cover of darkness to move unseen. I know how to hunt.

And I always catch what's mine.

Lena sits at the far end of a quiet rooftop bar, sipping from a glass of wine, her gaze locked on the view of the city below. She's beautiful like this— unguarded, unaware that I'm watching.

Unaware that no matter how far she runs, I will *always* find her.

I step forward.

She doesn't turn, but I see the way her shoulders tighten, the way her grip on her glass tenses.

She knows I'm here.

Good.

"Didn't take you as the type to drink alone, *gattina*." My voice is smooth, controlled—exactly the opposite of the storm inside me.

She exhales, tilting her head slightly, but still doesn't turn. "I was enjoying the silence."

I smirk, stepping closer, letting my presence wrap around her like a vice. "Then why does your pulse say otherwise?"

Lena

I should have known he'd come.

Hell, a part of me *wanted* him to.

I left because I thought I had to. Because I wasn't sure if what we had was real or just the byproduct of adrenaline, danger, and desperation.

But sitting here, feeling the weight of him behind me, the heat of his body even without touching me—I know the truth.

I never really wanted to run.

I just wanted him to chase me.

I take a slow sip of my wine, keeping my voice even. "You can't keep doing this."

"Doing what?" His breath is warm against my neck now.

"Hunting me."

He chuckles, dark and knowing. "You *want* me to hunt you."

A shiver dances down my spine, traitorous and electric.

"Admit it, Lena." His voice drops lower, a growl against my skin. "You missed me."

I exhale, setting my glass down with more force than necessary. "You're insufferable."

He moves before I can brace myself—gripping my wrist, pulling me to my feet in one fluid motion.

And suddenly, I'm *in* him. Pressed against the railing, caged in by Dante's heat, his hands bracketing my hips, his lips inches from mine.

"You think I'd let you go?" His voice is raw now,

filled with something dark and possessive. "You think I'd let you slip away after everything?"

My breath hitches.

His eyes—God, those *eyes*—artic blues—burn through me, demanding, devouring.

I should push him away.

I *should*.

Instead, I lift my chin, challenging him. "What are you going to do about it?"

DANTE

Her defiance is my undoing.

I slam my mouth onto hers, and she *breaks* against me—soft and wild, every bit as desperate as I am.

Her hands are in my hair, gripping, pulling, dragging me closer.

I growl against her lips, gripping her hips, dragging her flush against me until there's no space left between us.

She tastes like wine and fire.

Like something I'll never let go of.

I press her further against the railing, swallowing the gasp that leaves her lips.

"You ran," I murmur against her throat. "But you *knew* I'd come for you."

She shudders beneath me. "I did."

I smirk. "And now that I've caught you?"

She meets my gaze, fire and challenge and *something deeper*.

"You already know the answer."

I do.

She's mine.

. . .

LENA

Dante kisses me like he's claiming me.

Like I belong to him.

And for the first time, I *let him*.

Because the truth is, I don't want to run.

Not from him.

Not from *us*.

I curl my fingers into his shirt, pulling him closer, pressing my lips to his ear. "Take me home, Dante."

He stills, his breath ragged, his grip tightening.

Then, in one swift motion, he lifts me into his arms, carrying me away from the rooftop, away from the city.

Because we both know—

This isn't the end.

It's the beginning.

DANTE

She doesn't run.

Not this time.

And I don't let go.

Because *Lena Voss* is mine.

Review Request

*****

"Thank you for reading! If you enjoyed this book, I would be incredibly grateful if you could take a few minutes to leave a review on Amazon, Goodreads, Bookbub, etc.

Your feedback helps other readers discover stories like this, and it means the world to me. Just 30 seconds and a short comment can make a big difference!"

Click Here To Write A Review!

Sneak Peek!

A Triple Bonus! (1 of 3)

Did you love Lethal Obsession?
Then you should read SUSAN by Amanda
Shittim!

SUSAN

SUSAN   The Last Clue   A Romantic Thriller

SUSAN: I decode the world's most complex ciphers, but nothing in my career prepared me for this—a cryptic note falling from the pages of a rare book. A note signed with a single letter: **E**. There's only one person it could be from. **Ethan Park.** The man who vanished from my life five years ago, leaving me with nothing but unanswered questions and a heart that never fully healed.

Now, he's back, standing in the shadows of **San Francisco's Pier 39**, looking just as dangerous—and just as irresistible—as I remember. He tells me he's on the run, that he's uncovered something deadly, and that **I** am the only one who can help him crack the code.

I should walk away. I should tell him he lost that right years ago. But the moment the bullets start flying, I realize something terrifying—**I'm already part of this mystery.** And the only way out... is through him.

ETHAN: Five years ago, I let Susan go. I had my reasons—good ones. But I never stopped thinking about her. Now, with a target on my back and a story too dangerous to keep buried, she's the only person in the world I can trust.

I thought I was prepared to face her again. I was wrong. The moment our eyes meet, the past crashes into the present, threatening to pull me under. But there's no time for regrets. **Philip Kwan**, one of the most powerful men in Silicon Valley, is willing to kill to keep his secrets locked away. And unless Susan and I decipher the truth hidden in these encrypted files, we'll be next.

She doesn't trust me. I don't blame her. But the fire between us? It never died. And now, with danger closing in, I don't know what's more dangerous—**the people hunting us, or the way she still makes me feel.**

A heart-pounding romantic thriller

filled with secrets, betrayal, and a second chance at love neither of them saw coming. The biggest risk isn't cracking the code—it's trusting each other again.

Read more at www.amandashittim.com

Sneak Peek!

A Triple Bonus! (2 of 3)

Did you love Lethal Obsession?
Then you should read Whispers Between the Veil
by Amanda Shittim!

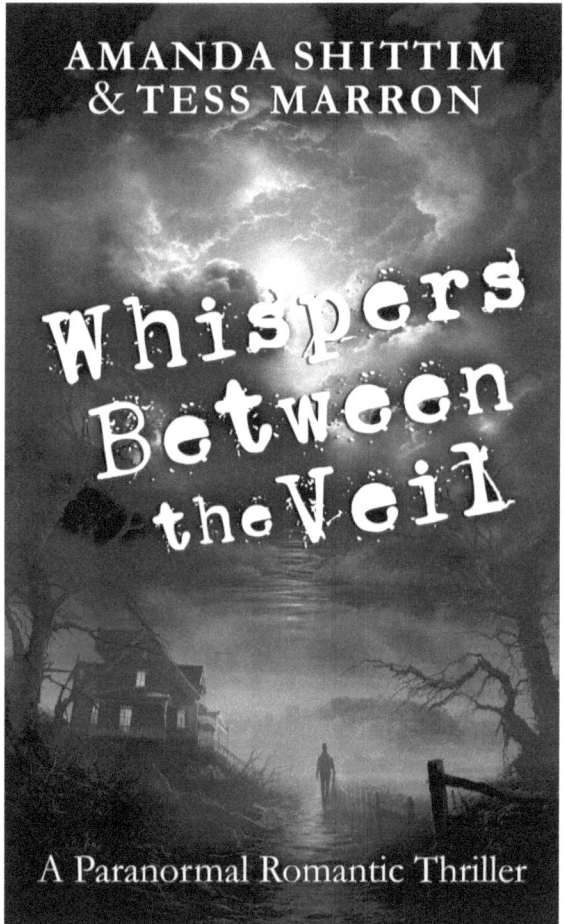

Whispers Between the Veil

In the crumbling shadows of Blackwood Hollow, a
troubled artist and a curious historian uncover a
love that defies time—and the dark secrets that
threaten to claim them both.

In the murky depths of Blackwood Hollow, along a long rural road, the old house stands alone, its wide porch creaking under the weight of years. The shingles on its roof curl in protest against the passage of time, and the acres of overgrown land surrounding it feel as though they've swallowed the land whole. I'm Emma Sinclair, and this dilapidated place has been left to me. It's a quiet refuge, or so I thought. What I didn't expect was to find myself tangled in the ghosts of a long-forgotten past, one that seems to reach out to me with every passing breeze.

I'm not the only one drawn to this place. Gavin Reid, a local historian, shows up at my doorstep uninvited. There's something about him—his intense gaze, the way he's searching for something in these ruins. He says he's here to learn about the history of the place, but it doesn't take long to realize he's not just interested in the house; he's fascinated by something much deeper. And before long, I find myself caught in the web of dark secrets he's uncovering.

Each night, the house seems to whisper to us—both of us, pulling us together in ways neither of us can explain. The air is thick with the tension of things left unsaid, with the weight of a love that never quite died, even if it's long gone. Gavin and I are tied to something beyond our control, and as we uncover more, the past begins to consume us. It's as if the house itself is alive, watching us, testing us. We can't ignore the pull between us, but every step we take seems to bring us closer to a tragic end.

I'm not sure if this is fate or something darker, but I know one thing: we can't escape Blackwood Hollow. Not until we face the love and the loss that still echoes in its walls.

Read more at www.amandashittim.com

Sneak Peek!

A Triple Bonus (3 of 3)

Did you love Lethal Obsession?
Then you should read A Girl's Best Friend by
Amanda Shittim!

A Girl's Best Friend

A sparkling heist, a forbidden romance, and a city shrouded in mystery.

In the enigmatic heart of New Orleans, where shadows dance to the rhythm of jazz and secrets linger in the humid air, Grayson Wolfe leads a dangerous double life. By day, he's a polished gem in the diamond trade; by night, a haunted former detective turned noble thief, waging a silent war against the city's criminal underbelly. Driven by ghostly visions of justice undone, Grayson walks a razor's edge between vengeance and redemption.

When Ava Sinclair, a sharp-tongued thriller author, finds herself framed for a daring diamond heist, her fiction collides with a chilling reality. Pulled into Grayson's treacherous world after an attempt on her life, Ava discovers a labyrinth of conspiracies, spectral whispers, and the dark allure of her reluctant savior.

As they delve into New Orleans' hidden secrets, deciphering cryptic riddles left by the dead, their partnership ignites with a passion as dangerous as the shadows stalking them. Together, they unravel a conspiracy that could cost them their lives—or set them free.

In this steamy, supernatural thriller, love, danger, and redemption intertwine, proving that even in the darkest corners, diamonds—and hearts—can shine.

Read more at www.amandashittim.com

My Heartfelt Thanks

THANK YOU TO A POWER GREATER THAN ME THAT DOETH THE WORK...

About the Author

Amanda Shittim is an emerging author of romantic thrillers. This is Amanda's first novelette and fourth book.

About the Publisher

Bridgewater & Buchner Publishing Co. is an emerging publishing house dedicated to bringing fresh, captivating romance narratives to readers worldwide. With a focus on discovering new voices and unique perspectives, Bridgewater & Buchner is carving a niche in the romance genre. Among its talented authors is emerging romance novelist Tess Marron, known for her evocative storytelling that explores themes of love, longing, and connection. As a rising name in the industry, Bridgewater & Buchner remains committed to delivering beautifully crafted stories that resonate deeply with readers. Read more at:

https://bridgewaterandbuchner.com